Princess Ponies

Season's Galloping

Princess Ponies

Season's Galloping

CHLOE RYDER

SCHOLASTIC INC.

ISBN 978-1-338-19453-1

12 11 10 9 8 7 6 5 4 3 2 1   18 19 20 21 22 23

Printed in China   68

This edition first printing, September 2018

With special thanks to Julie Sykes

The Pony

Queen
Moonshine

Princess
Crystal

Princess
Cloud

Princess
Stardust

Princess
Honey

Royal Family

King
Firestar

Prince
Jet

Prince
Comet

Prince
Storm

Chevalia

N
W   E
S

Horseshoe
Hills

Savannah

Grasslands

Canter's
Prep School

The Fields

Mane Street

Prologue

Hidden in the middle of the seas is the island of Chevalia, a magical place surrounded by golden beaches. It's ruled by the royal ponies Queen Moonshine and King Firestar from their court at Stableside Castle.

But a long way from Stableside, in the middle of the Horseshoe Hills, was a smaller, dilapidated castle with crumbling ivy-clad walls. Mice and beetles lived in the empty rooms. Bats roosted in the turrets and spiders hung from thick webs.

In a dark room with spots of damp peppering the walls, a mean-looking pony with a square nose was preparing to go out. She put on a black cloak and pulled the hood over her face. Next, she covered her hooves with foam-backed horseshoes. The pony, whose name was Divine, walked to the opposite side of the room, then trotted back. Her hooves made no sound on the stone floor.

"Perfect!" A wicked smile lit Divine's face. "No one will hear me when I walk down Mane Street to strip the Christmas tree of its decorations."

Reaching up, Divine unhooked a large sack from a nail on the wall. She hung it round her neck and went out through the back door. On silent hooves, Divine galloped to Mane Street.

While the ponies of Chevalia slept, Divine stared at the enormous Christmas tree, tall and proud at the end of the street. Its snowy branches were covered with horseshoe decorations that sparkled in the moonlight. Divine set to work, removing the horseshoes and hiding them in her sack. When the tree was empty, she brushed the stray pine needles and glitter from her cloak. A wicked smile lit her sallow face.

"Chevalia," she whispered, "I've ruined Christmas for you. Only when you accept me as your rightful queen will I stop thinking up ways to make your lives as miserable as mine."

Divine cackled softly as she galloped away, the tree decorations bouncing in her sack.

Chapter 1

Pippa MacDonald woke early. It was unnaturally quiet, and the room was bathed in a bright white light. Butter-flies danced in her stomach as she leapt out of bed.

"Snow!" Pippa's breath came out in a white cloud as she threw back the curtains and stared onto the street. "Snow for Christmas day."

On tiptoes, Pippa crept downstairs

to the Christmas tree. The fresh smell of pine needles tickled her nose.

"Wow!" she gasped. The tree stood in a sea of presents. Pippa's eyes traveled over the parcels, trying to guess the contents from their shape. So many of the gift tags had her name written on them, but had she gotten the present she wanted the most? "Please let there be ice skates!" Pippa had her heart set on a white pair that she'd seen in Tillingdale's department store.

Pippa couldn't wait for her family, Mom, Miranda, and Jack, to wake so she could find out.

Jack woke next. He ran around the tree shouting, "Choo choo!" He'd been hoping for a train set.

Miranda clumped down the stairs, grumbling. "Why so loud?"

"It's Christmas!" Pippa squealed.

"Presents, presents, presents!" Jack yelled as their Mom followed them into the front room.

"Can we open them now?" asked Pippa hopefully.

"Not yet," said Mom, her face serious. "There's been a change of plan. We're going to school."

"Good one!" Pippa laughed, thinking that her mother was joking. No one went to school on Christmas morning.

"It's true," said Mom.

"Ha ha ha!" Jack giggled.

"I'm sorry, kids, but a friend called me late last night. She's using the school kitchens and gym to prepare a Christmas feast for local people who aren't as lucky as we are. But she doesn't have enough helpers, so I said we'd go along too.

"Really? Suddenly I don't feel so lucky," said Miranda.

"I'm not going to school on Christmas day!" Jack jumped up and down. "No!" he shouted. "No. No. No."

"Yes," said Mom firmly. "We can all help out. And our Christmas can wait for a few more hours."

Pippa frowned. She didn't want to help either. But it seemed mean not to, especially when Christmas was supposed to be a time of good will.

After a hurried breakfast, they wrapped up in warm coats and winter boots. Jack was still being difficult, so Pippa volunteered to pull him on a sled. Mom was carrying two large bags filled with food.

"Why don't you pop them on the sled, Mom?" offered Pippa. "I can pull the groceries and the brother!"

Mom placed the bags in between Jack's legs and said, "Hold on to these."

"I'll eat it all up," he joked with a smile.

As they trudged through the snow on the familiar route toward school, Pippa pretended she was a reindeer pulling Santa's sleigh across the sky. But of course it was much harder to walk in the snow than fly through the air.

Still, Pippa loved hearing the crunch of the snow as her feet sank into it and seeing how the sled's train smoothed over her footprints as she pulled it. As they neared the school, they joined up with other parents and children. Many of them were also carrying bags of food.

"Cody!" called Pippa, catching sight of her best friend. She hurried across the yard and caught up to Cody by the frozen duck pond next to the gym. "Merry Christmas."

"Right back at ya," said Cody. She

pointed to a pair of ducks huddled together at the edge of the pond. "Look at them, poor things. The ice is so thick they've got nowhere to swim."

"They'll have to learn to ice skate," said Pippa. Her heart leaped with wonder. Had she gotten the ice skates she wanted?

The gym was buzzing with activity. Volunteers of all ages, wearing Santa

hats, were busy hanging decorations and setting the tables. In the school's kitchen, which joined onto the gym, a group of parents was singing as they prepared the Christmas feast.

"Mmm," said Pippa, her stomach rumbling in appreciation. "Something smells delicious."

"There's no time for daydreaming." Mom came up behind Pippa. "We've got a ton of work to do to make this day special."

"Yes, ma'am!" said Pippa smartly. She gave Mom a mock salute. "What can I do first?"

"Open the door," said Mom. She pushed her brown hair away from her face. "It's getting hot in here."

Pippa ran to the door and opened it

wide. A flurry of fresh snow rushed in on a cold breeze. Pippa opened her mouth to catch the snowflakes on her tongue. Most of them landed on her nose, making her giggle. Out of the corner of her eye, Pippa saw something gliding closer. She stopped catching snowflakes and stared in surprise.

It was a pony. A pony with wings.

"Princess Cloud?" Pippa blinked and rubbed her eyes. "Is it really you?"

Pippa couldn't believe that Princess Cloud would be here on Christmas day, but the ponies of Chevalia always found ways to surprise her.

Princess Cloud flew across the yard and hovered in front of her.

"Hello, Pippa," she said breathlessly. "I'm so glad I've found you at last! I flew to your house and knocked on your window with my hoof, but nobody was home. I followed the trail you left all the way here. I've come to take you back to Chevalia."

Chevalia was a magical island inhabited by talking ponies. Pippa loved visiting, especially to help her friends there sort out their problems, but today her heart sank. "Is something wrong? I can't come right now. I'm needed here, to make a special Christmas feast for people who wouldn't get one otherwise."

"You're very generous, Pippa, but Chevalia needs you too. It's Divine. We think she's up to her old tricks again," Cloud said persuasively.

"Then of course I'll come." Pippa suddenly remembered that time stood still in her world when she was in Chevalia. She could help both her pony friends and her human ones. She looked around to check that no one was watching; then she vaulted onto Cloud's back.

Pippa sank her hands into Cloud's soft white mane as the pony rose into the air. It was a thrill to fly over the snow-covered houses. Pippa tried to guess

what lay under the white blobs in people's yards. Before long, they reached the sea. Cloud raced across the ocean, her wings flapping rhythmically. Pippa leaned back, breathing huge gulps of the salty air.

"Chevalia," she whispered, as finally a small white dot appeared on the horizon. The first sighting of her favorite island always made her heart soar, and this time the island she loved was covered in snow!

As the dot grew larger, Cloud flew lower. Her hooves skimmed the snowy treetops of the Wild Forest as she flew toward the eight tall turrets of Stableside Castle. When the trees gave way to the plateau, Cloud banked away from Stableside, flying on to the collection of buildings on Mane Street.

Pippa loved Mane Street. It was the road where the ponies did their shopping, went to school, visited the fun fair, or just hung out together. "Oh look!" she breathed. "A Christmas tree! It's beautiful."

"It was beautiful," Cloud corrected her.

The tree stood at the far end of Mane Street. Its long straight branches were covered with glossy green needles that shone in the sunlight. Pippa was surprised to see that a crowd of ponies had gathered under the tree.

"Are they waiting for something?" she asked.

"Yes," Cloud continued. "Until last night, the tree was filled with silver horseshoes. There's a tradition here in

Chevalia. The royal family provide the shoes and the ponies of Chevalia decorate them. Today is supposed to be the day of the tree ceremony. That's when Queen Moonshine picks her favorite horseshoe. The winning shoe is placed at the very top of the tree. Then Queen Moonshine switches on the tree lights and there's a huge street party to celebrate."

"The tree ceremony sounds amazing," said Pippa. She hoped she could take part in it.

"It should be," said Cloud, lowering her head, "but not this year. Last night, while everyone was sleeping, someone stole the silver horseshoes. Every single one is gone. Christmas is ruined!"

Chapter 2

"Pippa!" said a familiar voice. "I'm so glad you're here."

A pretty pony with a long white mane separated from the crowd and galloped over to nuzzle Pippa in the neck. "Something dreadful has happened. Our horseshoes have been stolen!"

"Not again!" said Pippa, hugging Princess Stardust. "But at least this time the horseshoes are tree decorations, right? Not the golden horseshoes that hang on the Whispering Wall."

The eight magical horseshoes that hung from the stone wall at Stableside Castle were essential. Without their energy, Chevalia would fade away.

"They're not just tree decorations!" said Stardust impatiently. "They're royal tradition! Christmas will be ruined without them."

A hush fell over the clustered ponies. Suddenly they parted, making way for Queen Moonshine and King Firestar. The Queen, a dainty palomino with a golden coat and a snow-white tail so long it brushed along the ground, wore a deep red sash patterned with sprigs of holly. King Firestar, a tall copper-colored pony with bright eyes, wore a contrasting green sash patterned with robins.

"Your majesties." Pippa curtsied beside Stardust, her head bowed.

"Philippa MacDonald, here again when we need you most," said Queen Moonshine. Her dark eyes held Pippa's. "Without the horseshoes, we cannot have our tree ceremony. Please say you will find them and bring them back."

"I will!" Pippa promised. She loved Chevalia and would do anything for the island.

"Thank you." The Queen was relieved.

"We can always count on you," King Firestar added. "Our hero."

"Another adventure with my best friend," said Princess Stardust happily.

"I know exactly where to start our search. The Volcano."

"The Volcano?" asked Pippa. She wasn't so sure.

"Of course," Stardust rushed on. "See all those sooty black marks under the tree? That can only mean one thing. The Volcano Ponies have been here."

Pippa shook her head, her brown

curls bouncing as she protested, "The Volcano Ponies are our friends! They wouldn't steal from us. They're very shy. If they've been here at all, then they must have snuck out under the cover of darkness to see the tree."

"I'm sure it was them. I bet they were hoodwinked by Divine again. She probably made them steal the magical horseshoes. Divine keeps trying to spoil things for Chevalia."

Pippa recalled how Divine had tricked a couple of the Volcano Ponies into doing her bidding, helping her steal and hide the magical horseshoes that gave Chevalia its energy to exist. That seemed like a long time ago now, the first time Pippa had been called to help Chevalia, but she remembered that adventure like it was just yesterday.

"I don't know," Pippa protested. "The Volcano Ponies are clever, and I don't think they'd fall for Divine's tricks a second time."

"I still think it was them," Stardust repeated.

"It's not nice to accuse ponies without any facts to prove it, Stardust," said Pippa. "I tell you what: let's go visit them. We could take them some Christmas treats and then ask if they know anything about the missing shoes."

A familiar stubborn look crossed Stardust's face. Pippa waited quietly.

"All right then," said Stardust ungraciously. "If you insist."

"I do," said Pippa. "Thanks, Stardust. You're such a good friend."

"I am? Yes, I am," said Stardust. "Let's go visit the Mane Street Bakery. When I passed by earlier, Madame Colette had lots of tasty things in her window. We could take some to the Volcano Ponies. Everyone loves Madame Colette's cakes."

Madame Colette had a line of ponies stretching out the door. When she spotted Pippa and Stardust waiting at the end, she called them inside.

"Peeepa, Prrrincess Starrrrdust," she squealed. "Come in, come in, *mes petites*."

Pippa was learning French in school and knew Madame Colette was being friendly by calling them little ones.

"Have you come to buy the special cakes, baked by *moi*? Royalty comes to the front of the line, *c'est vrai?!*"

Pippa was embarrassed about skipping ahead in the line, but none of the waiting ponies seemed to mind. In fact, they all laughed as Madame Colette fussed and petted her, blowing in her hair and nuzzling her nose against Pippa's cheek.

She offered Pippa a square sample of cake.

"*C'est magnifique*," said Pippa appreciatively.

"*Merci*," replied Madame Colette. She was a pretty horse with a jet-black coat and bright rubies in her mane.

When Pippa explained that they

wanted to take a present to the Volcano Ponies, Madame Colette emptied her shelves of pastries and cakes. "The poor *petites*, stuck up there in that hot volcano. Go quickly. Take them my cakes while they are still fresh from the oven. I will bake more for the waiting ponies."

Pippa's mouth was watering as she and Stardust staggered out of the shop with boxes full of pastries. "We're never going to get these all the way up to the Volcano on our own! We need something to put them in."

"Tony Tack might have a hoofbarrow in his hardware store," said Stardust.

Pippa knew it would be nearly impossible to push a hoofbarrow up to the Volcano. But she did have an idea of what would glide over the snow.

"Look after these for a minute," she said. She left her cakes and pastries with Stardust while she dashed up Mane Street. Halfway along the road, she stopped next to a small shop with a large glass window.

"Eclipse's Sleighs." Pippa pressed her nose against the glass and stared at the display sleighs parked inside.

"Pippa!" Eclipse appeared by her side. "I thought I saw you! Welcome back to Chevalia. Have you come to buy a sleigh? I can make you a fabulous deal. I'll have you on the snow for next to nothing."

Pippa gave Eclipse a winning smile. "Actually, I was hoping I could make you a fabulous deal. Please would you lend Princess Stardust and me a sleigh, in exchange for a freshly baked carrot cake? We're off to visit the Volcano Ponies. We're taking them pastries as a Christmas treat."

"In that case, how can I refuse?" Eclipse whinnied. "But on one condition. Instead of giving me the carrot cake, you take it to my friend Night-shade. I haven't seen her since I moved down to Mane Street. I miss her so very much."

"Deal!" Pippa struck the bargain by patting Eclipse on the neck.

"Thank you, Pippa," said Eclipse. "I love Mane Street, and my new shop is doing extremely well. But I miss my old friends. They don't visit that often. They're so shy that Mane Street over-whelms them."

Pippa called for Stardust. When she trotted over, Eclipse showed them around to the sleigh lot at the back of her shop, where she helped them to pick a sleigh. "This one," she said, pointing to a smart purple sleigh in the corner. "It's not the biggest but it's the lightest, so it should be easy for you to both pull."

"Pull? Me?" Stardust was outraged.

"I'm not a common work horse. I am a Princess Pony."

Pippa laughed. She patted her friend kindly. "Of course you are, Stardust, but you're also going to help pull the sleigh."

"Princesses don't usually work," Stardust said. "I'll help this time. But only because we're looking for the horseshoes and I love having adventures with you!"

"Honestly, Stardust." Pippa laughed. "You should come and live at my house for a while and try doing my chores."

"Chores snores!" said Stardust. Then she tilted her head and whispered, "What's a chore?"

"A chore is a job you do when you're part of a family," Pippa replied. "My chores are raking the yard, helping to shovel the snow, folding the laundry, and picking up my room."

"Your life sounds hard."

"It really isn't," said Pippa, remembering the people that she was helping to make Christmas lunch for. "I'm very lucky. And so are you. Your life is too easy. Even royalty has duties and chores to carry out. Look how hard your parents work to make Chevalia the wonderful place that it is."

"Chores still sound like bad luck," grumbled Stardust, but she took her place beside Pippa as they pulled the sleigh, loaded with goodies, out onto Mane Street.

The sleigh was light and fast to pull through the snow, but as they climbed the Volcano the heat melted the snow away. It was much harder to pull the sleigh over the stony tracks that wound up the Volcano's sides. The nearer they got to the summit, the hotter the air became. Pippa wished she had something she could tie her hair back with, to help cool her down.

"Watch out," she squeaked, swerving to avoid a pool of molten lava.

"Are we nearly there?" panted Stardust. "It's so hot. My mane's sticking to my neck."

"Not far now," said Pippa encouragingly. "Whoa!" she gasped as they rounded a bend.

Ahead lay an enormous castle built into the black volcano face. From the slit-like windows, colored lights shone out. The turrets were decorated with tinsel and fake snow, and atop the tallest turret hung a sparkly gold star.

"It's so pretty," said Pippa.

"So was our tree, until the horse-shoes went missing," said Stardust wistfully.

Pippa's legs were aching. The sight of the castle gave her renewed strength, but as she was about to cross the huge wooden drawbridge, Stardust let out a triumphant squeak.

"Look! Sooty hoof prints. I knew it. The Volcano Ponies have taken our horseshoes."

Pippa stared at the black prints. It did look suspicious, but she still found it hard to believe that the Volcano Ponies would fall for Divine's tricks again.

"Stardust . . ." Pippa wanted to warn Stardust not to accuse the Volcano Ponies of anything without proper proof, but it was too late. The guards had seen them and were trotting over.

Chapter 3

The guards had smart red sashes around their necks and wore sprigs of holly in their manes and tails. Their coats sparkled with a dusting of silver glitter.

"Merry Christmas! Welcome to Volcano Castle," they whinnied. "Would you like a hoof with that sleigh?"

Pippa and Stardust nodded gratefully. In two shakes of a pony's tail, the guards helped Pippa and Stardust to pull the sleigh into the castle courtyard.

"Thanks," said Pippa, handing them each one of Madame Colette's pastries.

"Why are you giving them treats when they've taken our horseshoes?" whispered Stardust.

"Shhh," said Pippa. "We don't know that yet."

"Thank you. These are delicious!" The guards ate every single crumb as Pippa stared around.

"I'd forgotten how similar Volcano Castle is to Stableside."

"Except there's no Whispering Wall," Stardust pointed out.

The courtyard ended not in a huge stone wall, like the one at Stableside, but in a stone balcony that overhung a bubbling pool of lava. Pippa leaned against it and stared down into the golden pond. The heat from the lava was scorching, but overhead a wintry sky was visible through the top of the crater.

"Mmm." Pippa warmed her hands in the rising steam. "That feels good."

"Pippa, Stardust!" A little black pony galloped towards them. "What a lovely surprise! But why are you here?"

Pippa stared at Nightshade in

surprise. She sounded awkward. Was she hiding something?

"It's good to see you." Nightshade blew Pippa a friendly greeting through her nose. "How's my best friend, Eclipse?"

"Eclipse is fine and sends her love," Pippa answered. "She's started up a sled dealership. She's doing really well. She sent you a carrot cake."

"So Eclipse is a business pony now, a real big city pony!" Nightshade said with a smile. "The cake smells delicious. Come to my room. I've got a pot of hot apple juice on the stove that'll go nicely with it."

Pippa and Stardust followed Nightshade along a series of walkways. Pippa hadn't visited the Volcano for ages and walked slowly, taking it all in. The Volcano was even grander than she'd remembered. The walkways were lit with dark red candles with holly wrapped around the sconces. Pictures of ponies were carved into the black stone walls. There were caves of all sizes, some with stable doors, the top half open while Volcano Ponies went about their chores inside. Pippa noticed one pony sweeping up a stone floor and nudged Stardust to show her.

"See," Pippa said. "Everyone does chores."

"They're not royalty, though," Stardust replied.

Nightshade led the way to her cave at the end of a walkway. On the wall by the door was an ornate black spire with

a pony gargoyle atop it, wearing a red Santa hat. A golden torrent of molten lava poured from its open mouth. Pippa's nose wrinkled at the faintly eggy smell.

"We always decorate that statue with a Santa Hooves hat," Nightshade explained.

Next, she opened her stable door and led the way into a small, cozy cave. There wasn't enough room for the sleigh, so Pippa and Stardust parked it outside.

"Thank goodness," said Stardust. "My hooves can't go another step."

Nightshade began serving hot apple juice in small wooden troughs for the ponies and a mug, decorated with a picture of a girl, for Pippa.

Pippa cut the carrot cake and passed it around. While Stardust and Nightshade exchanged news, Pippa munched her way through three slices of cake.

"Pulling that sleigh made me hungry!" she exclaimed.

"Stardust, are you looking for something?" asked Nightshade.

Stardust jumped and drew her gaze away from a cupboard hidden in the wall. "The silver horseshoes," she blurted out. "Last night, they were stolen from the Christmas tree in Mane Street. We can't have our tree ceremony without them."

Nightshade stiffened. Hurt and anger flashed across her face. "So that's why you're really here. You think we've stolen your horseshoes!"

46

Stardust nodded. "Maybe not you, Nightshade, but the Volcano Ponies—"

"No!" Pippa jumped in. "We don't think that at all. We found sooty hoof prints under the Christmas tree, so naturally it made us think of the Volcano. We wanted to bring the Volcano Ponies a Christmas gift and thought we could ask if you knew anything about the

missing tree decorations at the same time." Pippa went to the door and pulled back the cover on the sleigh, revealing the boxes of pastries.

Nightshade blushed bright red. "Thanks. They look delicious. I know why you suspected the Volcano Ponies of stealing your horseshoes. A group of us secretly visited the tree in the night. We'd heard how beautiful it was, and we were too shy to go and look in the daylight. Whoever took the shoes must have stolen them after we were there."

"Oh!" said Pippa. "That explains the sooty marks. I'm sorry if we hurt your feelings. Stardust wasn't thinking straight. It's easy to jump to conclusions when you're upset. Now that we've solved that mystery, we can carry on with our expedition to find the horseshoes. Will you come with us, Nightshade? We could use your help."

"Me?" Nightshade was surprised. "Thanks, I'd love to. We don't get that much excitement up here. Come to think of it, we don't get any excitement up here!"

"That's great!" said Pippa. "Let's give out the pastries before we start."

Nightshade took them back to the courtyard, where she called the Volcano Ponies by banging on a huge copper gong. Soon ponies of all shapes and sizes crammed into the courtyard. Pippa, Stardust, and Eclipse unloaded the treats and handed them around. The chatter stopped. All that could be heard over the hiss of the lava pool was munching and whinnies of delight.

"Delicious! The best pastries ever."

"The apple ones are wonderful."

"Pecan nut and maple syrup for me!"

The Volcano Ponies couldn't stop thanking Pippa and Stardust for the tasty midmorning treat. When every single crumb had been eaten, they filled the empty pastry boxes with red lava berries and hoofed them back to Pippa.

"Take these to the Stableside ponies. Our lava berries make the best mulled lava-berry juice around," explained Nightshade, smacking her lips. "It's our Christmas specialty. I'll give you the recipe."

"I don't mind helping with this type

of chore," Stardust told Pippa as she helped with the boxes.

Pippa was getting impatient. They'd been at the Volcano for ages, and she was eager to get on with the search for the missing horseshoes.

"Where are we going next?" she asked.

"We could go to the Cloud Forest," suggested Nightshade. "Last night, on our way home, we saw a unicorn at the edge of the Cloud Forest. Maybe he saw something."

"Maybe he did!" said Pippa, brightening. "On we go!"

Chapter 4

With three of them to pull the sleigh, it didn't take long to reach the Cloud Forest on the eastern slopes of the Volcano. They stopped at the tree line, parking the sleigh in the shadow of a tall, snow-topped pine.

"Brrrr." Pippa shivered. "It's much colder here."

"Now I understand," said Stardust.

"What?" asked Pippa and Nightshade at the same time.

"Why the Volcano Ponies stay up here near the hot lava; it keeps them warm in winter."

Pippa smiled. "I told you they were clever."

Wisps of mist swirled among the snow-covered trees. Pippa's feet crunched softly in the snow as she entered the forest, ducking to avoid low-hanging branches and thick bundles of snow-clad vines.

"How do you know which way to go?" Nightshade asked as Pippa led the way.

"I'm following the hoof prints." Pippa pointed to a dainty set of prints in the otherwise pristine snow. "The unicorn that came this way wasn't wearing horseshoes," she added.

The mist thickened as they went further into the forest. It was quiet. Pippa breathed deeply, enjoying the silence and the freshness of the air away from the busy traffic and car fumes of her neighborhood. Gradually the snow became slushy and the ground beneath it felt spongy to walk on.

"We must be near the river," guessed Pippa.

Moments later, the trees thinned, and there was the riverbank.

"Wow!" said Stardust, taking it all in. "It's completely frozen."

The river could have been made from glass. Beneath the smooth surface, Pippa saw tiny red fish darting in and out of long green weeds.

"Will it hold us and the sleigh?" she wondered aloud.

Stardust tested it with a hoof. "It's solid," she said, "but it's very slippery. Be careful. Take it slowly."

With care, they made their way over the icy surface.

"This is fun," said Pippa, sliding her

feet along the ice. For a moment, she remembered it was Christmas morning back in her own world. Would there be a pair of white skating boots for her under the tree? Pippa hoped so. But if not, then at least she'd gotten to ice skate here in the Cloud Forest.

"How much farther?" asked Stardust, when they reached the other side. "My hooves are frozen."

"I don't know. You could try singing for Misty. She'll tell us if she knows where the horseshoes are."

Stardust looked uncertain. "I could, but what shall I sing?"

"How about a Christmas carol?" Pippa suggested.

"I don't know any Christmas songs about ponies called Carol."

Pippa hid her smile, "Never mind. I'll make a song up for you." She cleared her throat and began to sing.

Here in Cloud Forest, we came to see
Our best friend unicorn, called Misty.
We'll sing out loudly so she can hear.
Misty the unicorn, are you near?

Stardust joined in, and after a bit so did Nightshade, their voices rising to the treetops. They sang the song three times. Then, without warning, two unicorns burst out of the trees and cantered over to the frozen riverbank. Pippa recognized Misty immediately. It was uncanny how she looked exactly liked Stardust, even though unicorns were much smaller than ponies. Misty's magnificent spiralled horn in the center of her forehead was the only way to tell the two apart.

"Princess Stardust and Pippa." Misty and her companion, a black unicorn, curtsied.

Pippa glanced at Nightshade, then back at Misty's friend. "You must be Nightshade's unicorn double," she said.

"I am." The unicorn gave Nightshade a shy smile. Her voice was high and musical. "My name's Ashley, but my friends just call me Ashy."

"I have a unicorn double?" Nightshade was delighted. She blew a friendly greeting through her nose at Ashy.

"Every single pony in Chevalia has a unicorn double," said Stardust.

"Even Divine?" wondered Pippa. She shivered. Hopefully, Divine's unicorn double would be much nicer than she was.

"Are you here to sing with us?" asked Misty hopefully.

Stardust shook her head and explained the real reason for their visit.

"That's so sad." Misty's dark eyes watered. "I hate to think of your lovely

Christmas tree empty and bare. We haven't seen your horseshoes, have we, Ashy?"

The light danced on Ashy's horn so that it sparkled when she shook her head.

"I might have," sang out a deeper voice.

Everyone swung around to face a handsome-looking unicorn with a shiny, dark brown coat and black mane and tail.

"Hi, Blizzard," said Misty. "Do you remember meeting Princess Stardust and Pippa at Stableside Castle a long while ago on Midsummer Eve? This is their friend Nightshade."

Pippa bit back her impatience as introductions were made. "When did you see our horseshoes?" she asked as soon as it was polite to.

"Last night," said Blizzard, flushing as all eyes turned to him.

He spoke softly and Pippa leaned closer to hear as he explained.

"Something woke me and I couldn't get back to sleep, so I went for a walk. When I reached the edge of the Cloud Forest, I saw a group of Volcano Ponies heading home. By then I was wide awake. I stayed up to look at the stars. There was a fine moon and I could see for miles. A long while later, I heard clanking. In the distance, I saw a pony heading down the Volcano toward the Wild Forest. He carried a large sack on his back that was rattling and clanking with every hoof step. The pony had a

snowy beard, and at the time I thought he was Santa Hooves. That's why he was out so late at night. Perhaps it wasn't Santa Hooves after all, but another pony, the one who took your horse-shoes."

"Yes," said Stardust indignantly. "That's definitely our thief!"

"We shouldn't jump to conclusions," said Pippa gently.

"It's not nice to accuse someone of something they didn't do," added Nightshade.

Stardust blushed. "Sorry. I just want our horseshoes back before Christmas is ruined."

"We'll find them," said Pippa, patting her neck. "This is our first clue, and it's a great one. Good job, Blizzard. We'll leave you all in peace now and take our search to the Wild Forest."

"I'd like to come too," said Blizzard. "If that's all right?"

"Yes, please." Pippa was grateful for any extra help.

Misty and Ashy accompanied them to the edge of Cloud Forest. Then, wishing everyone lots of luck, they disappeared into the trees.

Pippa unhitched the sleigh. "To the Wild Forest," she said.

Chapter 5

The daring foursome—Pippa, Star-dust, Nightshade, and Blizzard—ran and galloped at full speed down the hill, the sleigh gliding over the snowy ground behind them. Pippa's cheeks were flushed with exhilaration when they finally arrived at the edge of the Wild Forest. It looked like a winter wonderland inside.

"That was fun," she panted, slowing to a walk.

"I loved it." Starlight's nostrils flared. "Pulling a sleigh's not so bad after all." She trotted into the forest.

"Careful," warned Pippa, noticing how the ground glittered with frost.

"Whoa!" Stardust's hooves slid from under her.

Pippa grabbed Stardust's mane, but her feet slid on the ice and she crashed into Nightshade. Nightshade skittered into Blizzard, and they all fell, landing at the base of a tree in a tangle of hooves and feet.

"Ooh, that hurt," said Stardust, rubbing her nose on her bottom. She struggled up and immediately slipped over again.

"How are we going to manage when the ground is so icy?"

"By going slowly," said Pippa. She stood up carefully, tilting her head as the clop of hooves came closer.

"Look!" said Nightshade, nodding.

Two Wild Ponies were trotting through the trees, their hooves flashing like fish scales in the winter sunshine.

"Nice horseshoes," said Pippa.

"What! They're ours! The Wild

Ponies did take our horseshoes," said Stardust hotly. She started to go after them. "Come back . . ."

"Stardust." Pippa put a hand on her mane to stop her. "You can't go around accusing ponies of stealing without proof. The horseshoes might be theirs."

"The Wild Ponies never wear shoes," Stardust protested.

"You still need proof," said Pippa. "Let's go and talk to them."

"All right," said Stardust grudgingly.

The Wild Ponies were fast on their hooves. Pippa, Stardust, and the others weren't so confident on the ice, especially with the sleigh to pull.

"We should have left it behind," panted Stardust.

They kept getting glimpses of the Wild Ponies, but each time they nearly caught up with them, the ponies started to run faster again. They seemed to be playing a tagging game. They were having so much fun Pippa wished she could join in, but it was difficult enough just staying upright on the slippery ground. Eventually, the Wild Ponies slowed. Pippa and her friends caught up with them in a clearing.

"The tree horseshoes!" squeaked Stardust indignantly, staring at the ponies' hooves. "They're definitely ours. The Wild Ponies stole them!" She trotted over to confront them.

The tall pony watched her warily. "Hello," he said. "I'm Stallyon, and this is Fusion. Who are you?"

"Don't you recognize her?" asked Fusion. "That's Princess Stardust with her girl, Pippa MacDonald." Fusion, a pretty pony with a strawberry-colored coat, stepped forward and dropped an awkward curtsy.

"Is it? I mean, it is," said Stallyon. He bowed his head. "What brings you to the Wild Forest?"

"You stole . . ." Stardust began, but Pippa quickly interrupted.

"Those horseshoes," she said, pointing at their hooves. "They're so sparkly. Where did you get them?"

"From me," boomed a familiar voice.

"Prince Storm!" Stardust was surprised to see her brother in the Wild Forest. Then she looked confused. "You did it? You stole the Christmas tree horseshoes? But why?"

Prince Storm was busy reacquainting himself with his unicorn double, Blizzard. "We sang together at the Midsummer concert," he explained to the Wild Ponies, bashfully adding, "Blizzard has an amazing voice, much better than mine. I prefer getting my hooves dirty on the farm to singing."

While Storm had been greeting Blizzard, more Wild Ponies came out from the trees to gather round the group. Pippa noticed they were all wearing shiny new horseshoes decorated with paint and glitter. She nudged Stardust, and her friend's eyes widened.

"Yesterday," Prince Storm began, "when I was taking a shortcut through the forest, I noticed how badly the Wild Ponies were slipping on the ice. It was alarming. It was only a matter of time before someone broke a leg." Storm paused to let the seriousness of the situation sink in. "I decided to go to the Grasslands and ask my friend Mucker— he's a farmer—if he would help me to make some horseshoes for the Wild Ponies to help them to stay on their hooves. On the way there, I saw something glittering in a bank of snow. Naturally, I was curious. Imagine my surprise when I dug into the snow and discovered a pile of horseshoes. I didn't realize they were the ones from the Christmas tree."

"It was you I saw!" Blizzard chuckled. "You must have gotten snow around

your mouth when you were digging. It made you look like Santa Hooves."

"Storm brought the horseshoes straight here and gave them to us," said Fusion. "There were enough for every Wild Pony in the forest. It made such a difference. We can travel around safely now."

"Pleeease can we keep the shoes until the ice melts?" Stallyon begged.

"But that could be ages!" squeaked Stardust. "What about our tree? We can't have a tree celebration if the tree is bare. Christmas will be ruined."

"Princess Stardust," said Storm gently, "remember your duty as a royal pony. You must help to look after all the ponies in Chevalia. The Wild Ponies need the horseshoes to protect them.

That's far more important than the tree celebration."

Stardust huffed out her breath. "I understand," she muttered. "But it doesn't seem fair."

"We all have to do things for others at times," said Pippa. "At home, my family and I were at school on Christmas day preparing a feast for people less fortunate than we are. But . . ." she added slowly, "I've got an idea. What if the Wild Ponies wore their new horseshoes to Mane Street? You could still have the tree ceremony, only everyone would be looking at the ponies' hooves when it came to judging the horseshoes."

"Wonderful!" Stardust started to laugh. It was so infectious that everyone joined in. Nightshade laughed so hard she nearly fell over.

"That's such a great idea, Pippa," finished Stardust when the laughter had faded. "We can start a new Christmas tree ceremony tradition right now! Line up, everyone: Royal Ponies, Volcano Ponies, Wild Ponies, unicorns, and girls. Let's do this properly. We'll make a real Christmas parade!"

There was a lot of noise and laughter as everyone got into pairs behind Pippa, Stardust, Blizzard, and the sleigh.

"Nightshade doesn't have a partner, so she should take the lead," said Pippa. "Then she can officially give the lava berries to the Stableside ponies. Ready? On we go!"

Chapter 6

Mane Street was packed with ponies all doing their last-minute Christmas shopping. As Pippa and Stardust pulled the sleigh down the middle of the street, word quickly spread that the missing horseshoes had been found. The crowds parted. Ponies lined the streets to cheer and point at the decorated horseshoes glittering on the hooves of Stallyon, Fusion, and the other ponies.

Pippa couldn't stop smiling. Mane

Street was the nicest place to be at Christmas. Strings of horseshoe-shaped fairy lights hung between the street lamps. The troughs were filled with sprigs of mistletoe and holly bursting with white and red berries. The shop windows were decorated for Christmas too. Mr. Gems, who owned the jewelry shop, had made a cotton wool snow pony decorated with jewels for his window; the beauty salon was draped with pink and gold tinsel; a delicious smell of freshly baked carrot pies drifted from Dolly's Tea Rooms, and the window was adorned with paper snowflakes.

The crowds thickened as they approached the Christmas tree, the ponies cheering loudly as the parade passed by. Only one pony, wearing a dark cloak with a hood covering her face, stood in silence. Pippa stared under the hood, and as their eyes met, she recognized the pony. Divine. Divine looked away, then melted into the crowd.

For a second, Pippa felt sad. She was almost certain that Divine had stolen the horseshoes. If only she could be

nicer! If Divine opened her heart to the ponies of Chevalia, Pippa felt sure they would open theirs back to her.

Pippa walked on to the huge Christmas tree at the end of the street where Queen Moonshine and King Firestar were waiting. The watching ponies fell silent as Pippa, Stardust, and Blizzard stopped a hoof step away and dropped into curtsies.

"Your majesties," said Pippa. "We have news of the missing horseshoes."

Slowly, with Princess Stardust chiming in, Pippa explained how they'd found the shoes. She pointed at the Wild Ponies, in pairs behind the sleigh, shyly shuffling their hooves. "So we hope," said Pippa finally, "that you won't mind not having tree decorations this year. And, that you will judge the horse-shoes on the ponies' hooves to pick a winner."

"Thank you, Pippa MacDonald," said Queen Moonshine. "I will happily agree to your suggestion. As for the Christmas tree, the ponies of Mane Street have been busy making new decorations with clay, glitter, and paint."

Pippa stared at the tree, her eyes widening in surprise. It was covered in decorations. There were miniature ponies, robins, tiny pastries, mini sleighs, baby carrots, and miniature toffee apples, to name a few. There were so many decorations they couldn't all fit on the tree, and many more had been piled around its trunk.

"They're beautiful," she gasped.

"It's the nicest tree ever," Stardust agreed.

Queen Moonshine and King Firestar walked down the line of Wild Ponies, examining each of their hooves and whispering to each other. Finally they returned to the Christmas tree. The crowd fell silent again.

"Fusion, please step forward," said Queen Moonshine grandly.

Blushing furiously, Fusion trotted over.

"I declare the winning horseshoe to be the one on your front right hoof. We love it because of the clever use of glitter and the star pattern. Congratulations. Will the pony who made this shoe please step forward?"

There was a lot of hoof shuffling

before a skewbald pony wearing a red and white neckerchief came forward.

"I'm Billie, Ma'am," she said, almost tripping over her hooves as she curtsied.

"It's a pleasure to meet you, Billie," replied the Queen. "Tell me about yourself and your creation."

Billie shuffled her hooves nervously, but two larger ponies nudged her forward.

"My folks are fairground ponies, your Majesty," she began. "And I made the horseshoe at Canters. Our teacher, Miss Huckleby, gave my class a whole afternoon to work on them."

"Well done, Billie. Your prize is a barrel of sugared carrots. In the past, we have always put the winning horseshoe atop the tree, but this year we shall break

with that tradition so that the Wild
Ponies may keep wearing all of their
shoes. So, as an extra prize, I shall give
your class a bushelful of chocolate-
covered carrots."

"Yay!" Everyone cheered, but Billie's
friends cheered the loudest.

"What about the top of the tree?"
asked Stardust. "We can't leave it bare."

"Quite right," said Queen Moonshine. She glanced over at King Firestar.

Clearing his throat, he held up a
winged pony carved from wood and
painted silver. "This angel pony was
made by Joey, Stableside's own car-
penter. Queen Moonshine has chosen
it to go on top of our tree. When the
decoration is in place, the street party
will begin."

Amid the cheers and whoops of delight, Cloud flew in and fixed the angel pony atop the tree.

Pippa threw her arms around Stardust's neck.

"Merry Christmas, best friend!"

"Merry Christmas," Stardust whinnied back.

The cheering faded away until

only a harsh cackling sound could be heard.

"What's that?" asked Stardust.

"Divine," said Pippa. "She looks furious."

"Silly ponies," Divine shouted. "Why are you all so happy when your tree is covered in junk instead of pretty horseshoes?"

Pippa walked over to her, "It's Christmas, Divine, a time of peace and good will to all people and ponies. Please come to the street party. Your old friends, the Volcano Ponies, sent lava berries for us to make into mulled lavaberry juice. I think you'll love it."

"No chance." Divine stuck her nose in the air. "Wild Ponies couldn't drag me there."

"Lucky for us, then," said Stardust.

Pippa gasped. "Stardust," she hissed. "That's not very nice. It's Christmas."

Stardust winked. "If Divine came to our feast she'd spoil all the fun."

A sly smile spread across Divine's face. "In that case, I've changed my mind! I shall come to your little feast."

"That was clever," Pippa whispered in Stardust's ear.

Stardust sighed. "Not really. I don't like Divine, but it's not nice to think of her spending Christmas alone. Let's take these lava berries to Dolly so that she can make them into mulled lava-berry juice."

Pippa had attended many feasts in Chevalia, but the Christmas street party had to be one of the grandest and happiest she'd ever attended.

"I can't believe how much there is to eat," she said.

"The Stableside Castle cooks have been preparing for weeks," said Stardust.

Pippa stared at the long troughs piled high with food. There was a mountain of honeyed oats, sugar-dipped apples galore, hot carrot pies, and Christmas pudding thick with cherries, but her favorite thing was the carrots carved into robins, bells, and Christmas trees. And of course, the mulled lava-berry juice.

"It's delicious," said Pippa, sipping the warm liquid from a goblet made especially for her. "It tastes like hot strawberry, cherry, blueberry, and peach all rolled into one."

Divine must have thought so too. Pippa was pleased to see her taking a long drink from a steaming trough full of mulled lava-berry juice. Divine had a sprig of holly in her mane, and for once she looked happy.

The ponies of Chevalia were lucky.

Many of them had been rescued from the human world because they weren't being looked after properly and didn't have enough to eat. Pippa wished she could feed all the people worldwide who didn't have much food either.

"Why so sad?" asked Stardust, nuzzling her arm. "Do you have to go home now?"

"Yes, but . . ." Suddenly Pippa had an idea. "Stardust, please could I have some of the decorations, the ones that won't fit on the Christmas tree?"

"Of course you can. What do you want them for?"

"Where I come from, some of the children hardly have anything. The little tree decorations would make lovely toys."

"Then you must definitely take all the spare ones," said Stardust. "I'll help you load them on the sleigh."

Word soon got around. As Pippa and Stardust piled the spare tree decorations onto the sleigh, the ponies came to help.

Pippa stood back and looked at the huge sack of toys.

"Are you sure it won't be too heavy for Cloud to pull?"

"Not if I use extra flying magic," said Cloud, hovering above it.

"I'll help," said Stardust. "Please, Cloud, please can I help to pull the sleigh?"

"And me," chorused Nightshade, Eclipse, Fusion, Stallyon, Storm, and Blizzard.

Cloud laughed. "You're all very welcome."

"A flying unicorn," said Pippa, after Cloud rubbed noses with Blizzard. "I've never seen one of those before!"

With so many helpers, the sleigh rose easily into the air. Pippa leaned over the side and waved good-bye to her pony friends.

"Merry Christmas, Chevalia," she called loudly.

"'Bye, Pippa! Merry Christmas to you," they neighed back.

Pippa waved until the island disappeared. She was usually sad when it was time to leave Chevalia, but this time she was excited, too. She couldn't wait to play Santa Claus. What would the children back home think of their new toys?

Chapter 7

Sleigh bells ring,
Voices sing,
As we bring toys
For girls and boys!

Pippa sang loudly as Stardust, Cloud, and the sleigh ponies flew over her school. Cloud chuckled as she guided the sleigh down, landing it in a secluded corner by the school gym.

"Thank you," said Pippa. Jumping

from the sleigh, she ran to each of the ponies and gave them a hug. At Blizzard she hesitated, because the unicorns were even shyer than the Wild Ponies. But it was Christmas, after all! To Blizzard's surprise, Pippa hugged him, too.

She saved Stardust until last.

"Merry Christmas, Stardust."

Stardust blew softly in her hair. "Merry Christmas, Pippa. Who'd have thought that doing chores could be so much fun! Come and visit us again soon."

"I will," said Pippa. "I promise I'll be back."

Pippa heaved the sack of toys from the sleigh and waved good-bye when Cloud instructed the ponies to take off. As they flew into the sky, Pippa rushed into the gym to find her mother.

"Thanks for opening the door, hon," said Mom, pushing her hair away from her face. "The cold air is very welcome."

"Door?" For a second, Pippa had forgotten that time stood still while she was in Chevalia. "Yes, the door. Quick! Come see what I found when I opened it."

"Steady, Pippa," said Mom, as Pippa pulled her outside. "My goodness! With those muscles, we should get you pulling Santa's sleigh!"

Pippa giggled. If only Mom knew that she had been dragging a sleigh around Chevalia!

"Oh my!" Mom stared at the sack of tree decorations. "What beautiful toys. There are some very kind people around."

"And some very kind ponies," whispered Pippa proudly.

As Pippa and her mom carried the toys inside, Mrs. MacDonald said wistfully, "All we need now is some music, and Christmas lunch will be perfect."

"I can do music," said Pippa. She climbed onto the small stage at the

front of the gym. The hall was packed with adults and kids. They turned to stare, and for a second Pippa's courage almost failed her. Then she remembered how lucky she was. She opened her mouth and sang.

Sleigh bells ring,
Voices sing . . .

The people in the hall fell silent, and as the noise faded Pippa heard a new sound coming from the roof.

As we bring toys
For girls and boys!

Pippa couldn't stop beaming as she sang along with her friends from

Chevalia, who were circling the roof to help her with her song.

Pippa sang three encores, then bowed to thunderous applause. A smiling Mrs. MacDonald helped her from the stage.

"Pippa MacDonald, you sure know how to surprise me!"

"Sometimes I surprise myself," Pippa replied.

"It's my turn now." Mom grinned. "I've got a surprise, too. Merry Christmas, honey!" Mom rummaged in one of her bags and pulled out a rectangular parcel. "I brought one present each for my kids to open."

Pippa stared at the wrapping paper covered with penguins and skating snowmen. Could it be . . . ?

Her fingers trembled as she carefully

peeled back the paper. Inside was a large box. Pippa opened the lid and pulled out pink-and-white tissue paper until she found a pair of bright white ice skates.

"Oh, Mom! They're beautiful." Pippa was so excited she could hardly speak. "I've wanted these for ages." Wrapping her arms around Mom, she hugged her tightly.

"Go on, then." Mom pushed her towards the door. "Take them for a spin."

"Thanks, Mom!" Pippa raced outside to the frozen pond. The ducks quacked as they flew out of her way.

With her skates on, Pippa stepped onto the ice and glided to the middle of the pond.

"Merry Christmas, Pippa!"

Pippa looked up as Cloud led the sleigh in a final circle above the school. Then, with a waggle of their wings, Cloud and the ponies soared into the sky.

"Merry Christmas!" called Pippa. "It's been my best Christmas ever, and it's not over yet."